DEATH SHIP OF THE ROACH PRINCESS

AUTHOR:
Matt Finch

EDITOR:
Jeff Harkness

LAYOUT:
Suzy Moseby

FRONT COVER ART:
Brett Barkley

INTERIOR ART:
Brett Barkley, Casey Christofferson

CARTOGRAPHY:
Robert Altbauer

PLAYTESTERS:
Kim George, Dan Delgado, Jeff Scifert, Levi Grear, Michael Nussbaum

ONLINE PLATFORMS COORDINATOR:
Sean King

FANTASY GROUNDS CONVERSION:
Michael G. Potter

FROG GOD GAMES IS:

BILL WEBB, MATT FINCH, ZACH GLAZAR, EDWIN NAGY, MIKE BADOLATO, and JOHN BARNHOUSE

FROG GOD GAMES

ADVENTURES WORTH WINNING

FROG GOD GAMES

ISBN: 978-1-6656-0167-2
SW PoD

Table of Contents

DEATH SHIP OF THE ROACH PRINCESS

BY MATT FINCH

A SWORDS & WIZARDRY ADVENTURE DESIGNED FOR A PARTY OF 3 TO 5 CHARACTERS OF LEVELS 1-3.

INTRODUCTION

BACKGROUND

Death-Ship of the Roach Princess is designed for a party of 3–5 characters of 1st through 3rd level. It is a completely freestanding adventure, but it can be used either as a prequel or sequel to *The Fiend of Turlin's Well*. The adventure begins with the characters about to investigate (and almost certainly becoming trapped on) *The Shifting Fortune*, a magical ship in the service of Teratashia, the demon-princess of dimensions and gaps. With the characters trapped on the ship, they risk being taken with it on a journey that — unless they stop it — ends their careers and destroys their souls.

Fortunately for the characters, the ship is not in perfect order at the moment because its captain, Torad Yarog, is out of commission. He disappeared on shore several days ago, leaving the crew in a state of disarray and delaying the ship's departure. If the adventure is played after *The Fiend of Turlin's Well* and Yarog escaped to the ship, his second-in-command has temporarily imprisoned him. Since this is only a contingent possibility, the adventure is written on the assumption that Yarog is still missing and that the crew has not yet located him. The section on the prison (**Area 14**) describes how to handle the "sequel-where-Yarog-escaped" contingency.

Even if the adventure is played after *The Fiend of Turlin's Well*, if Yarog did not escape the characters and return to the ship, the crew does not know his whereabouts. The crewmembers sent to find him are likewise still out of the ship even if Yarog returned on his own. They will find their way back, but not quickly enough to affect what the characters do while onboard.

A FEW NOTES

The arrangement of treasure in this adventure is very non-standard in that the vast majority of it is located in one place, quite early in the adventure. Since the characters have to deal with the fact that they are trapped, getting the treasure out is a problem — but they will know it's there for the taking if they can escape. Due to the way it's structured, moving through the adventure will seem less of an ordinary dungeon crawl (where each monster has treasure of some kind) and more like … something different. The impact of this adventure comes from the fact that it is unlike most other adventures in structure, content, and psychological feel, and the nonstandard placement of the treasure adds to this impression.

THE SHIFTING FORTUNE

The Shifting Fortune is a cursed ship that moves between gaps in realities. It is crewed by minions of the Demon-Princess Teratashia who gather information for the demoness, drop off her agents, supply her outposts, and deliver her eggs and spawn to hatch in many worlds. The ship is currently anchored in the harbor of a major city (Bard's Gate, if you are using the **Lost Lands** campaign setting), but its captain has gone missing. His second-in-command, a cleric of Teratashia by the name of Lyuul the Roach, is now in charge of the ship, so although the captain's absence has temporarily delayed departure, it will not keep the ship in port for very long. Lyuul eventually decides to abandon the missing captain and move onward to the ship's next port of call.

THE MISSING CAPTAIN

Torad Yarog, the ship's captain, is a fanatical follower of the Demon-Princess Teratashia (see the various appendices for more details on Teratashia and her minions). Torad is a doppelganger afflicted with multiple personalities, which is the reason for his absence from *The Shifting Fortune*. While he was on shore on ordinary business (ordinary, that is, for the captain of a cursed demon-ship), his personality underwent a shift from the one he calls "The Captain" into a rarer one called "The Fiend." In his personality of the Fiend, Torad went on a killing spree, entirely forgetting his responsibilities to the ship. The cleric Lyuul the Roach, the Fiend's link to Teratashia, assumes that Torad is still at large and dispatched some of the crew to find him.

THE TIMETABLE

Unless the characters prevent it from happening, the ship leaves in three days on its way to the nexus with an interdimensional tunnel at the Pillars of Draloon.

On the fourth day, the characters need to begin making saving throws to avoid joining the ranks of the cursed oarsmen.

On the fifth day, the ship arrives at the Pillars of Draloon and makes its transit into the gaps between reality. If the characters have not managed to stop its progress by this point, their fates are sealed and they are irrevocably lost in the spaces between realities, doomed oarsmen on the ship for eternity.

Adventure Start

If Played After The Fiend of Turlin's Well

If the characters played through the adventure *The Fiend of Turlin's Well*, they are most likely already investigating the ship and have some motivation to board it and find out what is happening. A quasit from that adventure may accompany them as well. The adventure does not require playing *The Fiend of Turlin's Well* first, however, as it is a freestanding module.

The quasit does not know about *The Shifting Fortune* (although he knows that such demon-ships do exist), but if the players are stuck, he can offer his thoughts based on his experience of the planes of existence.

> You have followed a grisly series of clues from Gaunt House in your search for the Fiend of Turlin's Well, and all evidence points to a ship called *The Shifting Fortune*. This ship, you discovered, is anchored in the port of Bard's Gate, and visible from the docks. From what you can tell, *The Shifting Fortune* is a rowed river-galley, with oars protruding from the side of the ship rather than having the rowers sitting on the top deck. You are gathered at the waterfront keeping an eye on the vessel and deciding what to do when a boatman pulls his craft nearby and shouts up to you, "Do you need a ferry out to one of the ships? I'm taking on passengers at a silver piece a head. Another silver if you've got more cargo than you can lift!"

If Played Without Previously Playing The Fiend of Turlin's Well

The characters are in a city located on a river port. Any city will do. Various rumors may lead the characters to investigate the ship, and these also provide them with the background information to understand a little bit of what is happening onboard the damnation-bound vessel.

> For the last week you have been knocking around the city's waterfront looking for interesting rumors. Most of what you've heard are the normal comings and goings of ships and cargo, but finally you've stumbled on something that's at least interesting, if not an offer of employment. Some of the longshoremen on the waterfront mention that one of their fellows brought a cargo of gold onto a ship called *The Shifting Fortune* and was going to do some more work for them. They haven't heard from him recently, though, so they can't give any more information on that. The longshoreman's name is Trout and as it turns out, no one seems to have heard from him in the last three days.

If the characters ask around a bit more, they discover that *The Shifting Fortune*, which is currently anchored offshore, is avoided by the various ferryboats and cargo lighters of the waterfront. No one can really say why, but everyone seems to have a bad feeling about the ship. If the characters inquire with the authorities, all records of the ship seem to have been misplaced, and the clerk is unwilling to go to the effort of rummaging around to find the paperwork. Other than the one mention of gold being brought onto the ship, no record explaining its presence in port seems to exist.

If the characters really dig into their investigation, they find that a few people have gone missing recently. No one has remarked on it since the population of a city's waterfront is a bit transient even under normal circumstances, but the more times the characters hear, "We haven't seen him in a few days," the more suspicious it begins to appear. Some of the missing people were boatmen who at some point made a delivery to *The Shifting Fortune*, but others seem to have no connection to the ship at all.

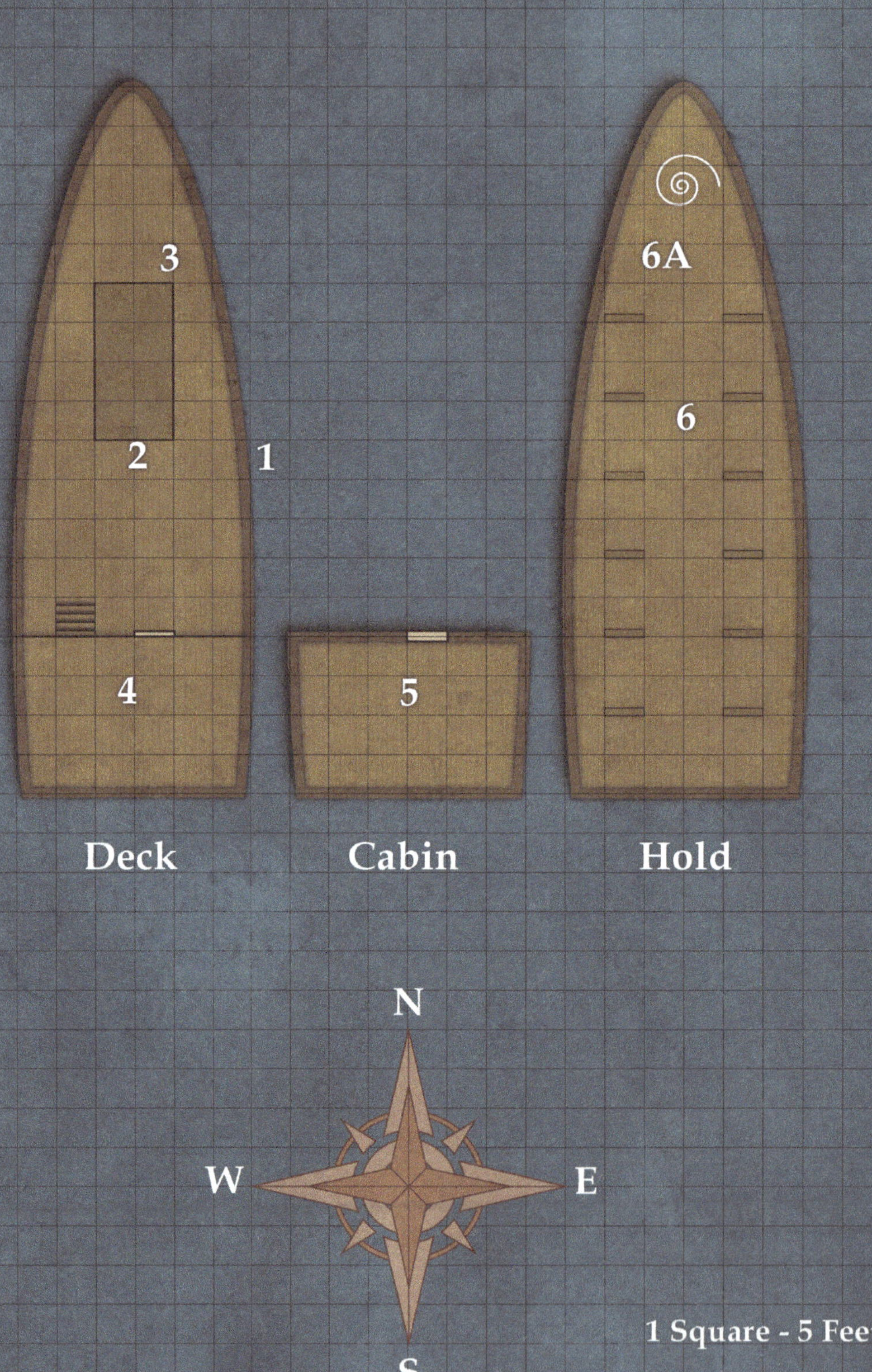

THE SHIFTING FORTUNE
3
2
1
4
Deck
5
Cabin
6A
6
Hold
N
W
E
S
1 Square - 5 Feet

Death-Ship of the Roach Princess

Approach

As you draw nearer to *The Shifting Fortune*, the city docks seem to recede quickly into the background and become shrouded in mist. You draw nearer to the ship at normal speed, but it is as if you are moving through a distortion of space, leaving more quickly than you are approaching.

The outer bulkheads of the ship have a blurred quality to them, and the lamps flicker slightly. No one challenges your approach, and you eventually draw near enough to see that the faint blurring and flickering lamps result from thousands upon thousands of roaches crawling in and out of the ship's woodwork and over the glass panes of the lamps. These are not swarms blanketing the ship, but far, far more insects than one would expect to see on a vessel of any kind.

The characters might make various preparations at this point depending on their general plan: stealth or frontal assault. At this time, they have already passed beyond the point of no return as they soon no doubt discover.

While it is not necessarily guaranteed, if the characters simply hired a boatman from the city wharf, the boatman panics and tries to bolt at some point because of the ship's supernatural appearance. He refuses to row the boat closer to *The Shifting Fortune* unless he is paid extra. Since he can't leave anyway (see below), this won't cause any inconvenience. Unless the characters engaged a brave boatman or approached the ship in some other way, read or summarize the following at whatever point the boatman would lose his nerve.

The boatman has been looking more fearfully at the eerie, silent ship. Suddenly, he begins to backwater with his oars, reversing course for the shore.

If the characters can't persuade the boatman to approach the ship by paying extra or by threatening him, read the textbox below when the boatman tries to get away:

The boatman starts rowing frantically away from *The Shifting Fortune* and makes good progress for the first several strokes of the oars. But after that, each pull on the oars seems to do less and less until the boat is motionless in the water. The boatman continues rowing, but the boat seems stuck in place, or perhaps making just a tiny motion forward. A gentle wave laps at the bow, and the boat is pushed back toward *The Shifting Fortune*. Once this happens, the process repeats: rapid movement at first, slowing almost immediately to a crawl and then to immobility.

The boatman keeps at this until he eventually gives up. Movement away from the ship at this point is governed by Zeno's paradoxes. The characters should realize they are trapped in a strange, altered dimensional space. (You may have to help the players arrive at the conclusion that what's happening is dimensional or planar, but a spellcaster in the party certainly arrives at this conclusion eventually.)

1. Climbing to the Deck

Since no one is on deck to let down a ladder or to challenge the characters' approach, they will have to get up the side of the ship to the deck. This is not difficult if they have a grappling hook (which no adventuring party should be without). If not, they will have to climb.

The only real feature on the side of the ship are the holes for oars since it is a rowed galley with the oarsmen below the main deck. It is likely that the characters peek inside one of these holes to see what they can see inside.

In the faint light that manages to penetrate the hole in the ship's side, you can see a person sitting inside the ship, their hands resting on an oar. They do not respond at all to the fact that you are looking in at them.

This is one of the cursed oarsmen described in **Area 6**. The person is alive, and if the character is loud or insistent enough, the oarsman turns to look dully at them. The oarsman will not respond any further, however. The characters have to enter **Area 6** before the oarsmen truly pay attention to them.

Roaches and Resting

Roaches infest the entire ship, including the strange, interdimensional gaps associated with it. They are everywhere, although in general they are not concentrated enough in mass to actually pose a danger. However, they are a constant feature, and it is worth mentioning them from time to time just to keep the imagery of the place in the players' minds.

An important fact, too, is that the presence of all these roaches crawling around is enough to keep anyone from sleeping or getting significant rest — unless the players think of a way to completely insulate a person from contact with the insects.

2. The Deck

The ship's deck is empty of people, but it crawls with roaches. A quarter-deck rises at the bow of the boat, with a door leading into it and a wooden stairway leading to the higher deck itself. A large opening leads to the belowdecks roughly in the middle of the ship's length. Five boats are near the railings, and a lantern is at the ship's prow.

The roaches on the ship's deck are not grouped together into the kind of masses that can actually harm people, but for every turn spent on the deck there is a 1-in-10 chance that a swarm coalesces and starts crawling onto and over the characters. The swarm is not dangerous.

Investigating the planking, railings, and other features of the deck turns up nothing other than a number of rat skeletons (these were killed and eaten by the roaches).

One of the boats is lashed to the railing and contains a 50-foot coil of rope. The others seem to be stacked haphazardly. A total of 15 oars are jumbled in with the boats. The lantern is lit and contains a pint of oil.

At some point very, very soon, the characters are going to attempt to leave the ship. Given that it's a very powerful demonic artifact designed — among other things — to catch and hold new slaves for the demon-princess, that's not going to happen without addressing the ship's supernatural power.

The ship swims in a dimensional space that essentially operates as a one-way door leading in. Getting onto a boat and rowing, or getting into the water and swimming, immediately runs into the spatial distortion surrounding the vessel. The boat (or swimmer) progresses a short distance from the ship, about five feet, and then progresses more and more slowly. That progress almost immediately slows to a crawl and then becomes so slow as to become nonexistent. Eventually some wave or wind tosses them back to the ship's side in a single sweep, forcing them to start over.

If the characters happen to have access to flying magic, they discover the same problem — a geometrical expansion of distance in one direction, and a geometrical compression of distance toward the ship. A flying character makes a bit of progress (although it's more like 40 or 50 feet), then slows, appears to hang in the air, and then eventually a stray gust of wind blows them backward.

In the extremely unlikely event that the characters have access to some type of dimensional magic, the same basic principle holds true, although in this case the "physics" of the situation are more like stretching a rubber band. The character makes progress quite well but then is forced backward by the dimension itself rather than by the random operation of wind or wave. The exact result differs according to the method attempted and is thus up to you to interpret, but there is a good chance that the character suffers damage as a result.

3. The Hole to Belowdecks

An opening in the deck exposes the ship's hold below. The opening is 10 feet across by 20 feet long and obviously designed for stowing cargo. It is covered by an iron grating, but this does not appear to be locked or fastened.

There is nothing magical or unusual about this opening or the grating. The grating is too heavy to lift, but it can be shifted sideways far enough to allow the characters to climb down into the ship's hold (**Area 6**).

4. The Quarterdeck

This higher deck is built over a cabin below. The ship's rudder would ordinarily be located on this deck, but there does not appear to be one. As far as you can tell, there is no way to steer the ship. There is, however, a lantern mounted on a pole. The lantern is lit.

There is nothing abnormal about the lantern, although it is almost out of oil.

5. The Cabin

This cabin space is empty and filled with dust. When you open the area to the sunlight, dim as it seems, you startle thousands of roaches massed on the floor and ceiling. With a clattering, chittering noise, they form together into a roughly human-shaped creature.

The steersman for the boat is formed from roaches. If it is given orders, it performs them but cannot leave the ship's upper deck. It attacks if it is not given orders. If the **composite roach demon** hits a target, it begins to smother the victim, inflicting 1d4 points of damage per round unless the victim makes a saving throw to escape.

Composite Demon (Roach): HD 2; **HP** 13; **AC** 4[15]; **Atk** smother (1d4); **Move** 9; **Save** 16; **AL** C; **CL/XP** 4/120; **Special**: resist bladed weapons (50% damage), smother (1d4 damage every round after successful hit, save avoids continuous damage; damage ends if demon is killed or attacks a different opponent).(see **Appendix B: New Monsters and Hazards**) **Treasure:**

The composite roach demon has no treasure. This adventure is unusual in that most of the treasure is in one location (the crates in **Area 6A**). Of course, for the characters to get the treasure out of the ship, they have to explore, fight, and think their way through areas a lot deeper than the treasure's location.

6. The Oar Deck

The air in the belowdecks is musty and foul. As with most oared galleys, the deck extends the entire length of the ship, with benches for rowers. Faint sunlight spikes in through the holes for the oars, illuminating the dust-filled air. Ten oarsmen are sitting quietly on the benches. The oars are pulled into the ship and rest across their laps. The oarsmen pay no attention to you when you enter, keeping their hands on the oars and their eyes straight ahead.

There are 10 cursed oarsmen in this part of the ship. They respond only if anyone talks to them directly, at which point they focus on the speaker with dull eyes. They are capable of intelligent speech, but it is halting and slow. They are not chained to the oars, but their hands are melted into the wood and they cannot be rescued by the simple expedient of breaking their chains — their captivity here is far more powerfully supernatural than mere physical constraint.

The oarsmen probably offer the characters the first warning that they are in real trouble. When the characters make some attempt to free the oarsmen — which is likely — the interaction probably leads one of the captives to let the adventurers know what they have gotten into.

The oarsman speaks slowly and dully. "You can't free us. We're damned. Cursed. You'll be like us soon. Give it three or four days, and you'll be sitting here at these oars just like we are."

The oarsmen understand things only from the perspective they have seen, and they aren't experts on demons or the supernatural, so their explanation, when questioned, is very vague.

"We got here different ways, mostly because we were hired as crew. I brought on some crates of cargo and got stuck here. I don't even know if anyone's looking for me onshore. I doubt it. But you can't leave. Can't swim back, can't hail the shore, can't do anything to get away. You start feeling lifeless, and then you start getting hungry and thirsty. You start to realize that touching the oars feed you and slake your thirst. Then it becomes a compulsion. And then finally you end up attached to them, with the wood melting into your flesh. You become part of the ship. You're looking at your future, friends."

The characters may ask about the ship's layout, and they can get bits of help from some of the oarsmen, although not much.

The fact that the cylinder (**Area 6A**) can be used to "leave" the ship:

"That cylinder of crates over there, with the passageway through it, that's a doorway. I went through it, but I couldn't find a way out. I don't have any words that can really describe it. You'll see what I mean."

The fact that the ship's crew inhabit the area belowdecks:

"The ship has a crew, but they don't come out here much. They're all on the inside of that cylinder of crates there at the ship's bow. They're human … I suppose. They don't look exactly right, if you know what I mean."

The fact that the ship's captain is currently missing:

"I'm the latest one here; I came aboard with a delivery, one of those crates, just three days ago. I went through that cylinder of crates, and I explored a little bit. I was sneaking around, and I heard two people — I guess they were people — talking about the captain of the ship. They were wondering where he had gone and thinking about sending a party ashore to look for him. Then they heard me, and I ran."

The **cursed oarsmen** are not capable of fighting, and if the characters attack them, it will be nothing more than a dismal slaughter gaining no experience for the characters.

Cursed oarsmen (10): HD 1d6 hp; **AC** 9[10]; **Atk** none; **Move** 6 (but held in place by the oars); **Save** 18; **AL** N; **CL/XP** A/5; **Special**: none.

6A. The First Interstice

A large, cylindrical arrangement of small crates is here, stacked like bricks all the way to the deck above. It is apparently arranged internally as some kind of spiral, for it would be possible for a person to walk into the cylinder. You can't see very far into it since the opening curves inward counterclockwise.

This is the characters' first encounter with one of the interstices — gaps — that riddle the supernatural space occupied by the vessel of the Demon-Princess Teratashia. It is indeed possible to enter the spiral one person at a time, and when the adventurers eventually do so, they will begin to understand the ship's unusual nature.

There is no significance to the fact that some of the interstices turn clockwise and others counterclockwise, but you will find that it is useful for distinguishing which of the interstices they are talking about once they start exploring.

Experimenting with the Interstice Size.

The spiral of crates is 20 feet in diameter, and it is possible to walk around it although it requires a bit of a squeeze between the crates and the sides of the ship. Whatever passage is taken past the internal spiral can't go around more than one or two circuits before running out of space.

Probing. The characters probably poke items into the gap, shine lights into it, and generally attempt to find out if it is safe to enter, whether anything is hidden inside, and so forth. There is no trap or danger involved with the interstice other than where it leads. If the characters cast *detect magic* on the spiral, they find that the entire thing is magical, but that the source of the magic is much stronger down the internal "passageway" than it is upon the crates and the entrance.

Disassembly. The characters may try to take apart the structure by removing crates from it. They find that the crates are extremely heavy, and — much more disturbing — anyone who removes a crate from the assembly loses 1d4 points of strength until the crate is put back in place, at which time the ability score returns to normal. The arrangement of the crates was part of a considerably powerful magic ritual, and undoing the structure saps power from the immediate area — specifically, the character doing the disassembly.

Opening the Crates. There are 100 huge crates forming the cylinder. Each of the crates contains 10 ingots of iron (worth 1 sp each), 5 ingots of silver (worth 1 gp each), and one ingot of gold (worth 10 gp each). The problem, of course, is that there's no way to get them off the ship unless the characters manage to stop the ship's progress into the gaps between dimensions.

Through the Interstice. Walking into the spiraling passage within the cylinder is to walk into a gap in reality. Each interstice in the ship leads to tiny pockets of reality caught in between larger and more significant realities. The first interstice leads to **Area 7**.

You enter the narrow space between the high-stacked crates, a passageway that immediately begins to curve in a counterclockwise direction. As soon as you make your way around the first curve, you notice that wooden skulls — carvings of human skulls — now start to appear as part of the structure in addition to the crates.

Assuming that the characters continue after whatever experimentation they do with the skulls (which are indeed wood and have the same magical characteristics as the crates), they emerge from the interstice into the carven passage (**Area 7**).

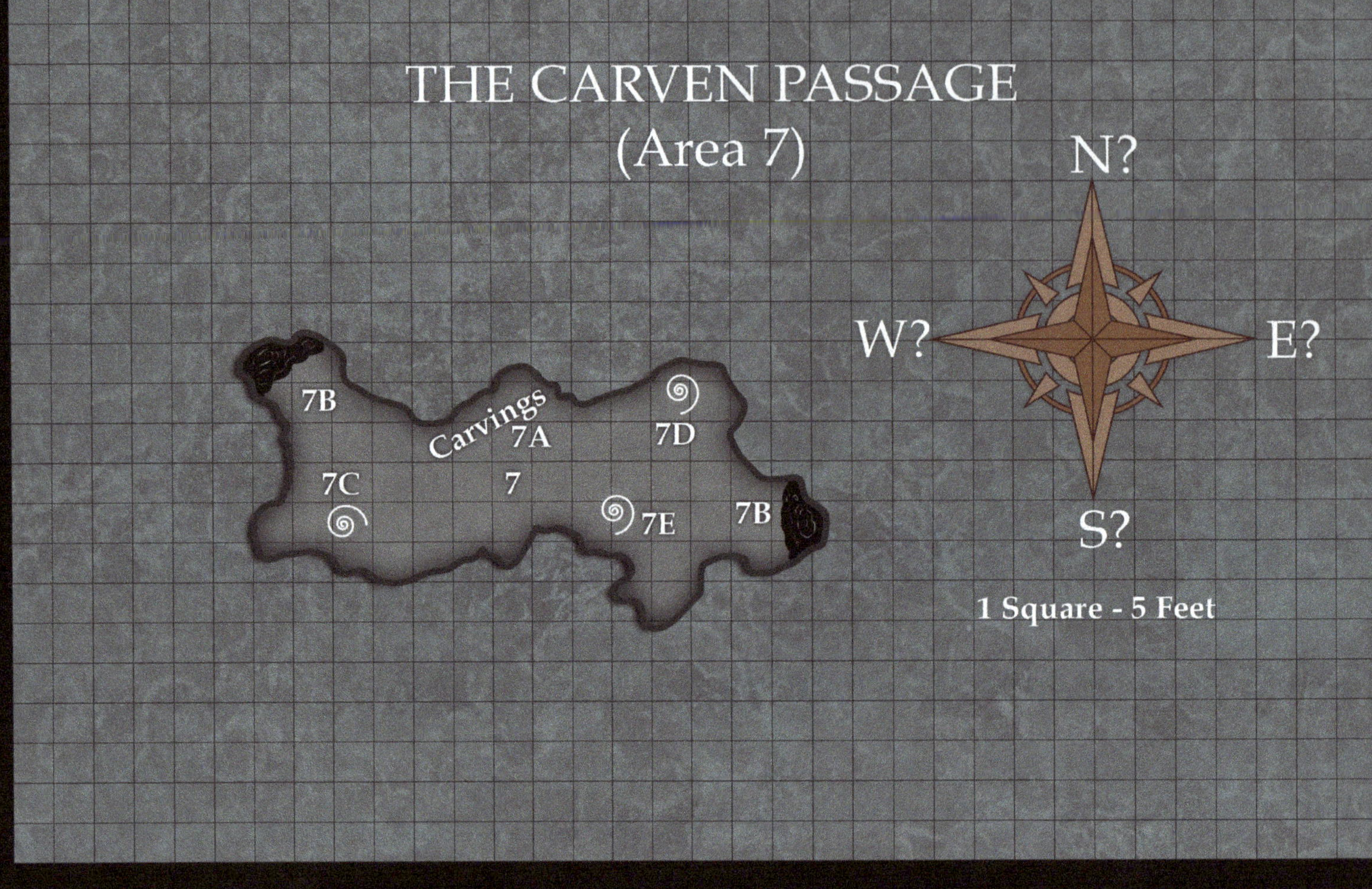

7. THE CARVEN PASSAGE

As you continue winding your way into the cylinder's internal spiral, you have now made almost one full turn inside. At this point, the passageway opens out into a stone chamber, apparently inside the cylinder but far, far too large for that to be possible. You are looking out into a long, underground cave with carvings on what ought to be the north wall. There are two apparent exits from the chamber, but they bubble with tar-like goo that fills the openings from floor to ceiling. There are also two cylinders strongly reminiscent of the one you are still standing in. These two, however, are built entirely of human skulls, and these don't look like carved wood. They look very real, the bleached bone reflecting in the light filtering in from the deck outside. Outside? You're not even sure.

7A. THE CARVINGS

The carvings on the chamber's north wall — perhaps north, anyway, since you can't be sure where you are — show at the center a huge, female-headed cockroach with a feral visage who is wearing a necklace of human skulls. The figure is surrounded by the outline of what might be a castle, but the line defining the castle-shape has so many gaps in it that it almost looks like a series of long dashes rather than a continuous line. Several of the gaps in the outline are marked with symbols. The most common symbol is a ship, and the next most common symbol is a cockroach. The other symbols do not repeat themselves more than once.

The other symbols include the following: people crawling, boxes, buildings, and a king or queen (it isn't clear which). Note: None of the ship-pictures are exact representations, so the characters won't be able to find one that looks exactly like *The Shifting Fortune*.

The carving is itself a symbolic representation of Teratashia's palace in the Abyss. While it has some qualities of a map if it is used correctly, it is utterly incomplete since the palace of the demon-princess literally defies the rules of geometry, logic, and reason.

A cleric is able to recognize the imagery and can recall reading a dusty old page from their days as an acolyte that described Teratashia (see **Handout A**).

7B. Tunnel Exits

This looks like it was once a tunnel leading out of the cavern you are in, but about five feet into the passage, the entire area is filled with what looks like slowly-bubbling black tar. It does not seem to give off any heat, but what it does give off is a sense of extreme dread. You can barely manage to look at it without chills running up your spine. Something is fundamentally wrong with the substance on a supernatural level.

The substance filling the tunnel is non-matter itself, the raw material of *spheres of annihilation*, the pure essence of destruction (see **Appendix B: New Monsters and Hazards**).

7C. First Interstice (From Area 6A)

This is the entrance into the cavern from which the characters emerge. It can be retraced to the ship at **Area 6** without difficulty — it is a two-way passage. The outside and entrance to the interstice — on this side — are made of human skulls. It is the only interstice built with crates and wooden skulls.

Refer to **Area 6A** for details on the interstices.

7D. Interstice to Area 8 (Counterclockwise)

This is a cylinder of human skulls with a narrow opening about three feet wide leading into it that immediately spirals counterclockwise into the structure.

The cylinder and its component skulls are similar to the other interstices. Refer to **Area 6A** for details.

7E. Interstice to Area 9 (Clockwise)

It may be noted by the players from the description that this cylinder turns clockwise rather than counterclockwise, but this information is of no importance other than as a way of keeping track.

8. Honeycombed Chamber

You are entering a stone chamber in which the walls are deeply honeycombed with gaps, holes, and cracks, looking almost like some kind of delicate, petrified lacework. A magic circle is incised deeply into the stone of the cavern floor. Like most magical circles, the perimeter is surrounded by runes, but the circle is very unusual in that it is not an unbroken line; it has a number of gaps that are obviously intentional.

This area is used to reach the ship's control chamber, which can be done only by teleportation using a set of command words the characters can discover if they proceed deeper into the weird, planar structure of the ship.

If the words "Yamatar, Vothontar, Uanibaster" or the words "Yamatar, Uanibaster" are spoken in this room, the gateway to **Area 15** opens (see below).

The middle word, "Vothontar," is supposed to be left unspoken other than in the mind, and failing to do so sets off a trap (described below). The gateway still opens if the words are all said aloud, but if "Vothontar" is spoken aloud, it sets off the trap.

Trap

If the trap is set off by speaking the word "Vothontar," the chamber begins to fill with tiny pinholes of unreality that cause damage to anyone in the room. The damage begins at 1 point of damage in the first round, increases to 1d2 points of damage in the second round, and remains at 1d3 points of damage per round for the remaining eight rounds of the effect's 10-round duration. Speaking the word a second time during the trap's duration causes the effect to stop, but speaking it again after the trap's effect stops sets the trap off a second time.

The Gateway

When (or if) the characters return to this chamber in possession of the magic words to open the gateway, and speak the words (whether activating the trap or not), the character who speaks the words, and anyone in physical contact with them, is teleported to **Area 15**. This can create a problem if the character speaking the words is the only one who has them written down. It is up to you, based on the experience of your players and the way you run your game, whether to assume the characters memorized the words or whether to confront them with a "Klaatu barada nikto" challenge.

8A. Interstice to Area 10 (Counterclockwise)

Walking through this interstice leads to **Area 10**.

8B. Interstice to Area 11 (Clockwise)

Walking through this interstice leads to **Area 11A**.

9. Stable of the Intellect Divulgers

Three large alcoves are in this room, like stables for massive horses. Each of them contains a horrid creature: a massive, exposed brain mounted in the back of a huge cockroach the size of a horse but roughly four feet tall.

Two of the tall, spiraling cylinders of human skulls are also in this chamber.

This room is a castoff in the dimension of time rather than the dimension of space. It shows various fragments of time that are of recent significance — significant at least in the mind of the rudimentary intelligence of the ship itself.

The three roaches are intellect divulgers. Their stables are unconnected to the dimension of the ship except visually, so nothing can reach in or out of the stables, and the creatures represent no threat.

On further inspection, a bas-relief image is carved in the stone beside each one of the stables: a feral face on a bipedal cockroach that is wearing a necklace of skulls. One of the skulls of each carving has two deep eye sockets. Placing fingers into both eye sockets simultaneously causes the intellect divulger to show the latest memory it was instructed to recall. The room is used to preserve details of conversations.

9A. Entrance Interstice (from Area 7E)

This is the interstice through which the characters initially enter the chamber, from **Area 7E**.

9B. Interstice to Area 12 (Counterclockwise)

Walking through this interstice leads to **Area 12**.

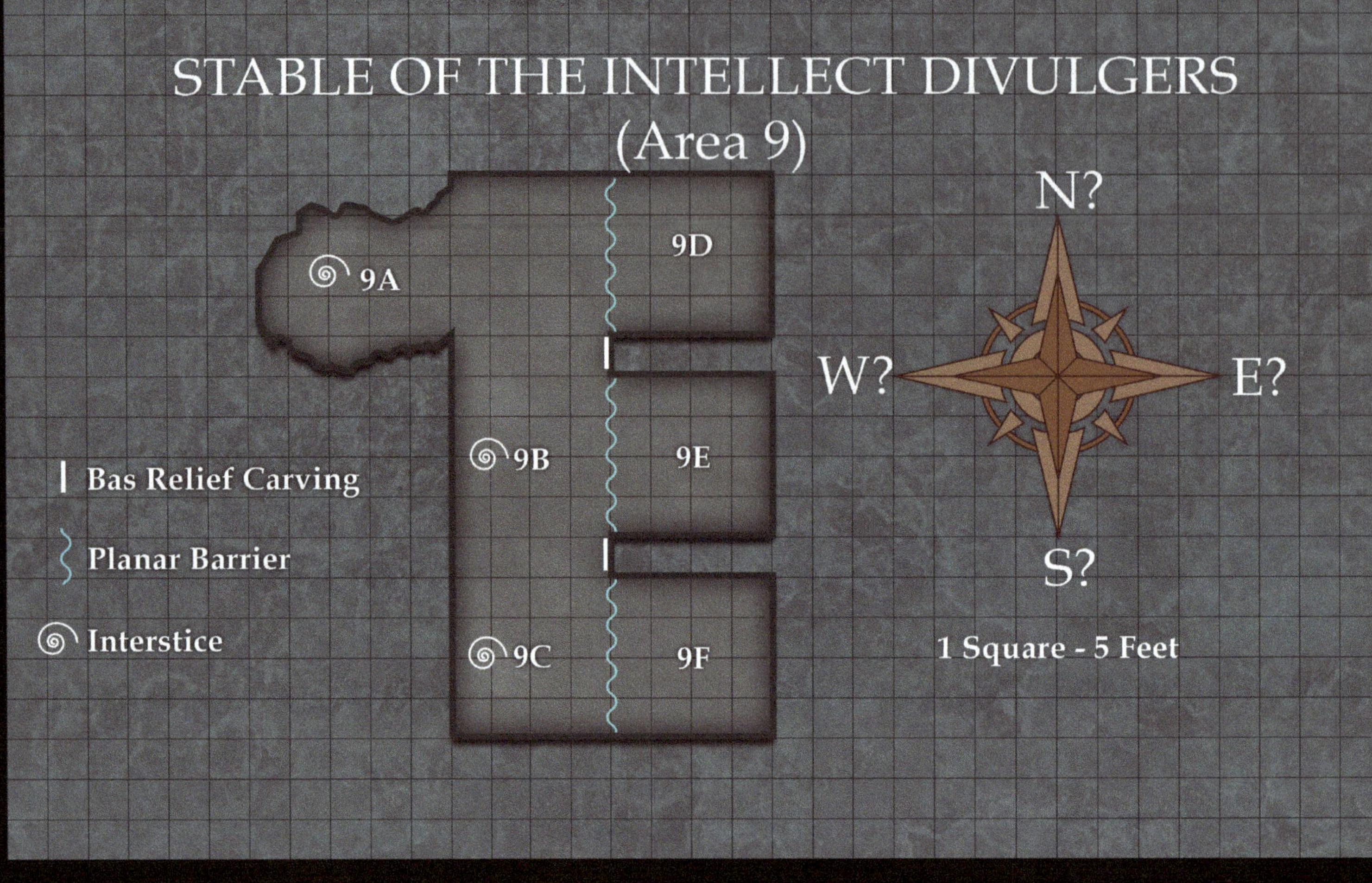

9C. Interstice to Area 13 (Clockwise)

Walking through this interstice leads to **Area 13A**.

The Stable-Alcoves

Pressing fingers into the eye sockets of the bas-relief carving outside any of the three stables causes an image to form around the intellect divulger.

> The giant, roach-shaped creature suddenly appears to blur around the edges as threads of multicolored mists snake outward from the exposed brain to form an image around the creature.

9D. First Intellect Divulger

The image that can be summoned from this intellect divulger may be described as follows:

> The image that forms around the enormous roach-creature shows two humans talking to each other. One of them is dressed in red robes with a wide collar embroidered with skulls, and the other wears a hooded robe. The face beneath the second person's hood appears to be shifting slightly; your first impression is that its expression keeps changing, but you then realize that the facial features themselves are altering as the person talks.
>
> The first figure, the one with the collar of embroidered skulls, begins talking as if midway through a conversation: "… This is dangerous. How do you know that your mind won't alter itself while you are ashore? We should send some of my cultists to find them, not send the captain. You know that your self is stable while you are on the ship, but if you leave the gap and enter the world, there is no telling what will happen."
>
> Before the hooded person can answer, the image fades away, dissolving back into threads that recede into the roach-creature's exposed brain.

9E. Second Intellect Divulger

The image that can be summoned from this intellect divulger may be described as follows:

9F. Third Intellect Divulger

The image that can be summoned from this intellect divulger may be described as follows:

10. Cultist Chambers (Entrance)

This area is an underground crypt from a different world that broke away from its original reality as part of a consecration service once the chambers were filled with interred bodies. The cultists of Teratashia discovered the place floating in the nothingness of unreality and assimilated it into their interdimensional tunnels.

Any character with a religious background can guess that the paintings and symbols are dedicated to some kind of tomb-guardian, but it is not a being with which they are familiar. Details on the deity to whom the area was consecrated — Charon of Far Kathan — are provided in the Appendix in case a character has access to divination magic.

The interstice in this area can be used to move back and forth between here and **Area 8A**.

The tarry mass is non-matter, identical to that found in **Area 7B** (see **Appendix B: New Monsters and Hazards**).

10A. Cultists' Sleeping Chambers

These are the sleeping chambers of **2 cultists of Teratashia** (see **Appendix B: New Monsters and Hazards**). The skeletons are left from the tomb's initial use, and the cultists have not bothered to remove them. The skeletons are not animated and represent no threat. If examined after the characters eliminate the cultists, the skeletons are human, but the bones have strange proportions (the humans are not from this dimension).

The cultists are human, although they look subtly wrong due to the fact that they are not native to this actual dimension. They fight with a berserk frenzy and do not surrender. If they are knocked unconscious and questioned, they are not forthcoming with information for they are utter fanatics. However, some bits of fragmentary information might be gleaned from their spitting fury at their captors.

- The ship is in the service of the Demon-Princess Teratashia.
- The ship travels through the gaps in dimensions, gathering information for the demon-princess and stealing what it can find to bring back to her as tribute
- The oarsmen are gathered by the ship, which is essentially a trap, and almost always die during the trips through various holes and tunnels in the dimensions. They are more like expendable fuel than crewmembers. Every one of the oarsmen is doomed.

Cultists of Teratashia (2): HD 2; HP 14, 10; AC 5[14]; **Atk** mace (1d4+1); **Move** 9; **Save** 15; **AL** C; **CL/XP** 2/30; **Special**: none. (see **Appendix B: New Monsters and Hazards**)
Treasure: The room is remarkable for its lack of any personal effects belonging to the people who live here. Not only is there nothing of value, but there aren't even any of the ordinary valueless items one would expect to find here.

10B. Dining Room

The pantry is a noisome cabinet of filth. It contains rotted foodstuffs swarming with maggots, piles of what looks to be roach excrement, and other even less palatable things.

10C. Empty Quarters

CULTIST CHAMBERS
(Area 10)

As with the rest of the cultists' chambers, this tomb area has been turned into living quarters for the ship's crew. The beds in this chamber have not been used recently, for it is occupied by crewmembers who were sent to find and retrieve the ship's captain. A ranger can make an educated guess that the chamber has not been occupied for at least five days.

10D. Empty Quarters

This room contains a pair of beds, but it looks uninhabited. The walls of the chamber are painted with old, faded religious symbols of some kind. The south wall — you think it's south, in any case — has had an altar or some other kind of fixture removed from it, since there is an area bare of any painting or symbols.

This room was ordinarily inhabited by two of the ship's cultist crewmembers, but (as with the ones from **Area 10C**) the crewmembers are currently on shore looking for the ship's missing captain.

10E. Roach Demon Room (and Interstice to Area 13B)

This room contains a cylinder like the others you have encountered, crafted of human skulls with a narrow opening about three feet wide, immediately spiraling counterclockwise inward. As you look into the room, thousands of roaches swarm out from the cylinder to form a human-like shape.

This room is guarded by one of Teratashia's **composite roach demons**, which attacks anyone who enters the room.

Refer to **Area 6A** for details on the interstices.

Walking through this interstice leads to **Area 13B**.

Composite Demon (Roach): HD 2; **HP** 15; **AC** 4[15]; **Atk** smother (1d4); **Move** 9; **Save** 16; **AL** C; **CL/XP** 4/120; **Special**: resist bladed weapons (50% damage), smother (1d4 damage every round after successful hit, save avoids continuous damage; damage ends if demon is killed or attacks a different opponent). (see **Appendix B: New Monsters and Hazards**)

10F. The Secret Cargo

A long corridor leads from the entrance hall, with four burial niches along the righthand wall. A vague smell of rot fills the corridor.

The burial niches in the "west" wall contain skeletons (not animated ones). If the characters search through the niches, they find only a few worthless trinkets interred with the bodies. If they search for secret doors, however, they may discover one of the most disturbing secrets *The Shifting Fortune* holds: its true cargo.

The four secret alcoves of this area each contain a large egg placed in the center of the alcove and surrounded with rotting meat, the source of the smell. These eggs contain demons, the spawn of Teratashia. They are dropped off in various worlds the ship visits to create agents and loyal servitors of the demon-princess. The eggs are worth 250 gp each, but anyone willing to buy one of them is most certainly not the sort of person

CLERIC'S QUARTERS
(Area 11)

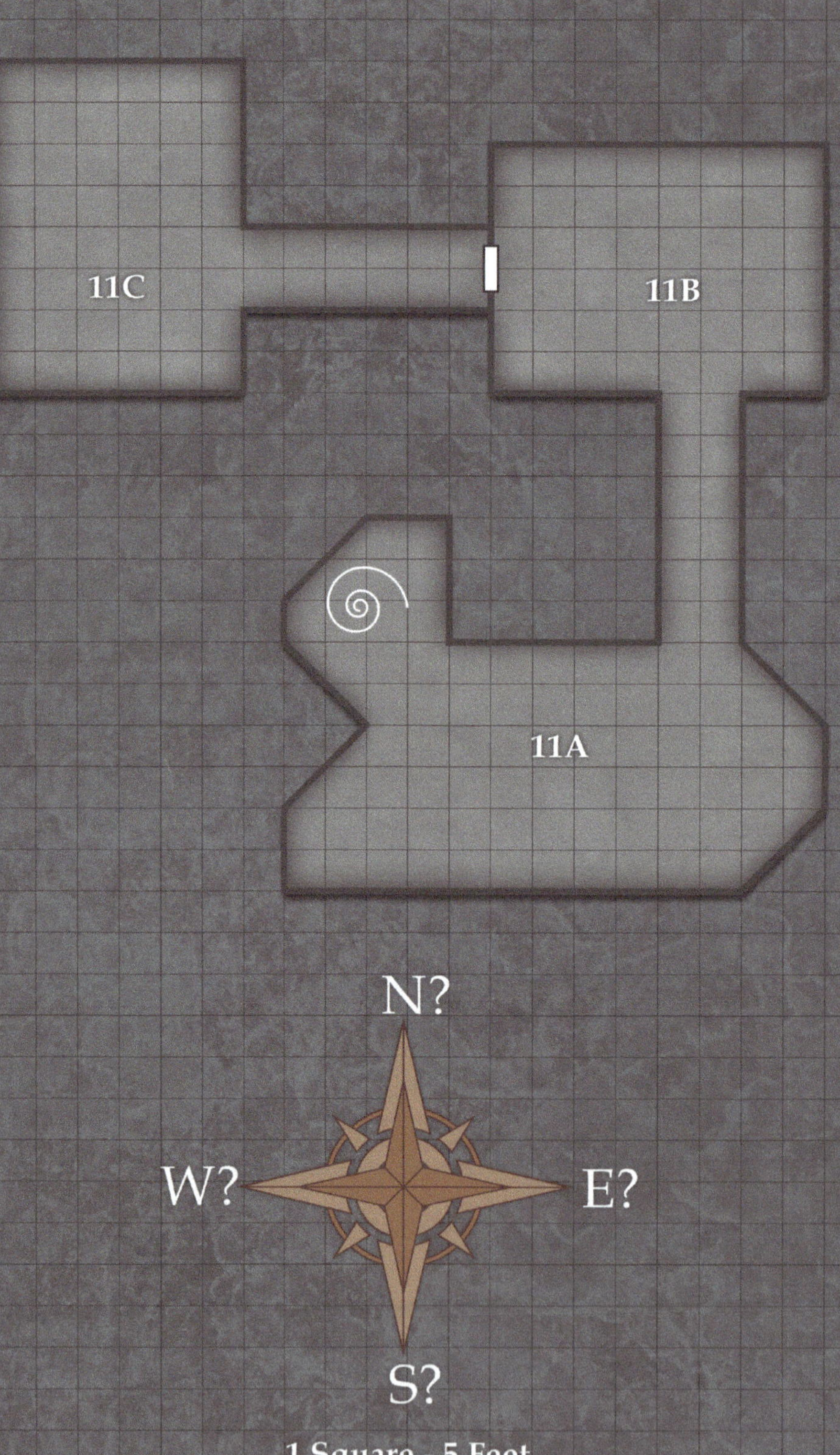

a heroic party would want to sell them to. If the characters escape with the eggs and choose to destroy them, they have struck a relatively significant blow against the demon-princess.

10G. Crypts

This corridor contains burial alcoves along the right and left walls. The alcoves are five feet deep and five feet wide, and each contains a skeleton wrapped in a burial shroud. At the end of the corridor, a black, tar-like mass appears to be oozing from the wall.

The skeletons in this crypt are not animated.

The tarry mass is non-matter identical to that found in **Area 7B**. Touching the black tar causes a character to take 1d6 points of damage, or half that amount if the character makes a saving throw. A second exposure causes 2d6 points of damage, and a third causes 3d6 points of damage, and so on.

10H. Crypts

Burial alcoves are cut into the stone along both sides of this corridor.

The cultists don't use this part of the old crypt. The burial alcoves contain skeletons (non-animate), but nothing important is in the area.

11. Clerics' Quarters

The passageway from **Area 8B** leads into **Area 11A**.

11A. Entrance

Emerging from the cylindrical passage, you see a room that is clearly inhabited, although there is no one in it at present. The walls are paneled wood, the stone floor is carpeted, and there are two comfortable-looking chairs, and a writing desk. The room is lit by a single candle burning in a candlestick on the table.

From the entrance, the characters cannot see the passageway in the northwestern portion of the room. If they make noise before seeing it, they alert the cultists in **Area 11B**.

11B. Guard Post

This room contains two cots and a table. A door is in the room's left-hand wall, which appears to be riddled with holes about one inch in diameter.

Two cultists are here, guards for the cleric Lyuul the Roach. While intruders are the last thing they expect to run into, they are relatively alert due to the honor of their position. They are alerted to the party's presence by any noise issuing forth from **Area 11A**. If this happens, their first reaction is to warn Lyuul in **Area 11C**.

Cultists of Teratashia (2): HD 2; HP 13, 11; AC 5[14]; Atk mace (1d4+1); **Move** 9; **Save** 15; AL C; CL/XP 2/30; **Special**: none. (see **Appendix B: New Monsters and Hazards**)
Treasure: Between them, the cultists carry 5 gp and 16 sp.

11C. Cleric Lyuul the Roach

This is the bedchamber of **Lyuul the Roach**, a cleric of Teratashia who is currently in command of *The Shifting Fortune* due to Torad Yarog's unexplained absence. If the cultists in **Area 11B** are alerted to the characters' presence, they immediately warn Lyuul. He hears any fighting in **Area 11B**, so it is highly likely that Lyuul reacts long before the characters enter his chambers.

This is a luxurious bedchamber with a four-post bed, two comfortable chairs, a wardrobe, and a large chest.

The wardrobe contains three sets of ordinary clothing and a set of red robes with a broad collar embroidered with human skulls, together with boots and other ordinary items one would expect to find. Nothing here is magical.

The chest contains 20 pieces of parchment, two bottles of ink, quills, some sealing wax, a religious symbol of Teratashia, a devotional book of some kind, and, at the bottom, a small stone tablet.

The devotional book is filled with obviously demonic prayers to the Demon-Princess Teratashia, including the following as a representative sample (**Handout B**):

"For Teratashia is the Princess Between, the watcher where there is nothing, the traveler in emptiness, the crawler of wormholes, the finder of lost places, Demon-Princess of the Unseen.

She rules the spaces where naught exists, the pathways through nothing, and finds the ways between.

She watches, listens, finds, takes, feeds, with feral face and chitin wings, for she is the Roach Queen."

The following is written on another of the parchment sheets (**Handout C**):

"Ship to take passage through the Pillars of Draloon and thence into the Gap of Gestria. Upon the death of the oarsmen in the Gap, thence to the Underworld of Maug, to deliver the souls and take on cargo of portable holes ..."

The following is written upon the stone tablet (**Handout D**):

"Bedoriomedes. Omniphonologon. Anjoole."

The tablet is also inscribed with a sigil or rune of some kind.

These words are the key required to enter the captain's chambers at **Area 12**.

Lyuul the Roach, Male Human Priest of Teratashia (Clr3): HP 15; AC 3[16]; Atk heavy mace (1d6); **Move** 12; **Save** 12 (+1, ring); AL C; CL/XP 3/60; **Special**: +2 save vs. paralysis and poison, banish undead, spells (2). **Spells**: 1st—*cure light wounds* (x2).
Equipment: chainmail, red robes with wide collar embroidered with skulls, heavy mace, *+1 ring of protection +1* (with a silver roach carved atop it), unholy symbol of Teratashia, 2d6 gp.

CHAMBER OF THE FIEND
(Area 12)

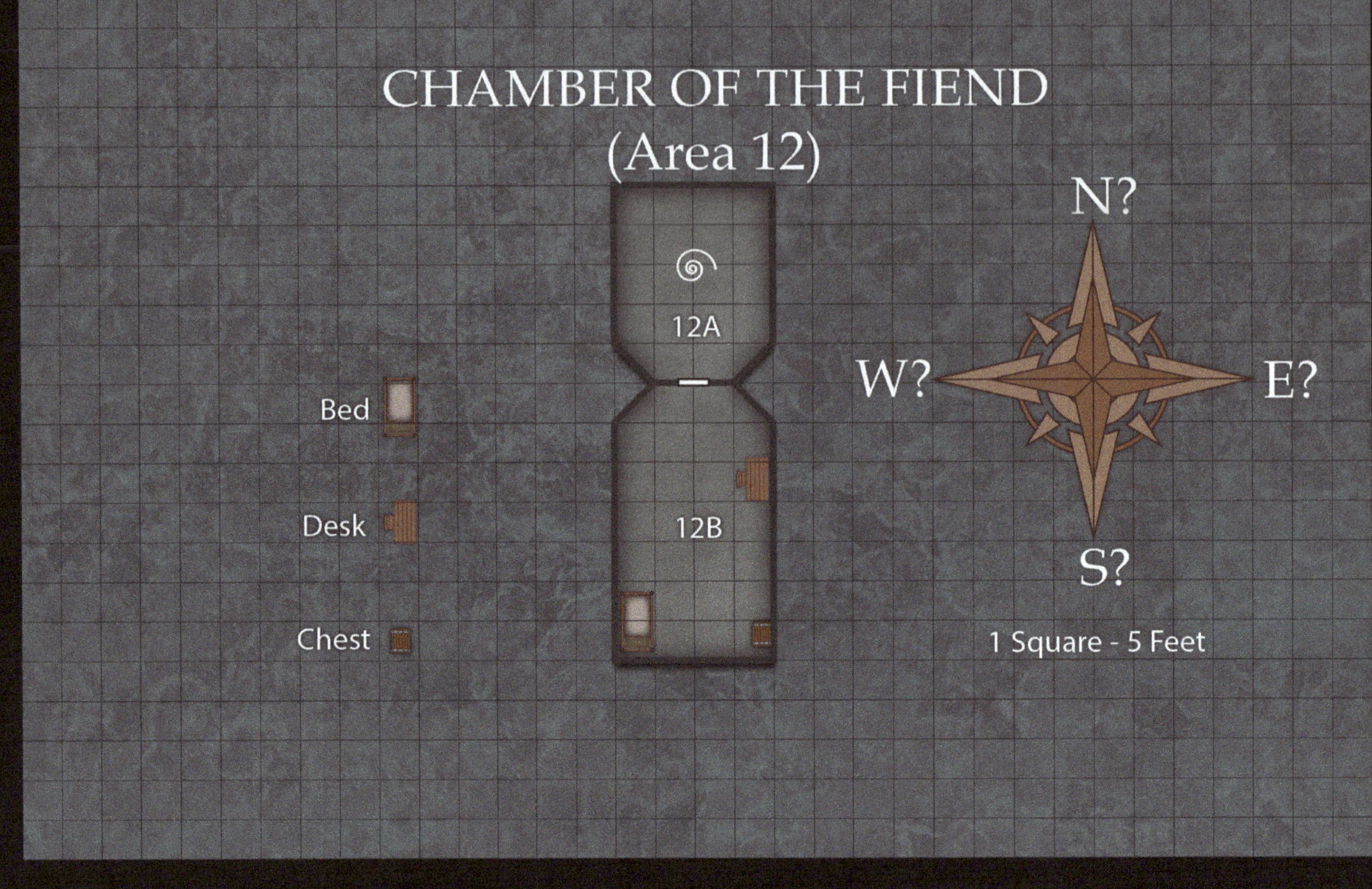

12. Lair of the Fiend

These rooms are the quarters of Torad Yarog, the ship's missing captain, whom the characters may have encountered while playing *The Fiend of Turlin's Well*.

The passageway into this area enters at **Area 12A**.

12A. Antechamber

The passageway opens out into an unfurnished and undecorated stone chamber facing a metal door encrusted with verdigris.

The door cannot be opened unless the required words are spoken. These words are found on the tablet in the chambers of Lyuul the Roach (**Area 11C**).

The required words are "Bedoriomedes. Omniphonologon. Anjoole." In addition, there is a right and a wrong way to speak them. The middle word, "Omniphonologon," must be left unspoken (other than in the mind) in order to avoid setting off a trap. The door opens even if the words are all said aloud, but if "Omniphonologon" is spoken aloud, it sets off the trap.

Trap: If the trap is set off by speaking the word "Omniphonologon," the chamber begins to fill with tiny pinholes of unreality that cause damage to anyone in the room. The damage begins at 1 point of damage in the first round, increases to 1d2 points of damage in the second round, and remains at 1d3 points of damage per round for the remaining eight rounds of the effect's 10-round duration. Speaking the word a second time during the trap's duration causes the effect to stop, but speaking it again after the trap's effect stops sets the trap off a second time.

12B. Bedchamber

The door opens into a bedchamber sparsely furnished with a desk, a chest, and a bed. A number of sketches drawn on parchment are nailed to boards on the wall to your right.

The walls contain sketches of eight people, all of whom bear a great deal of similarity to each other. Each sketch represents one of the Fiend's multiple personalities. Seven of the personalities are drawn beautifully by an expert hand, but the eighth is a crude sketch. The sketches are all labeled: The Artist, the Fiend, the Loyal Follower, the Questioner, the Wanderer, the Liar, the Captain, and the Pleasant Fellow. The crude sketch is of the artist, the only one the artist personality did not make.

The room has obviously been temporarily vacated. Three sets of clothes are tossed onto the bed, and a chest in one corner has been left open. Some empty hooks are on the wall, and others contain articles of clothing. A set of artist's tools is scattered on a desk, and an empty easel stands in another corner.

The key to entering **Area 15**, where the ship can be "deactivated," can be found on the desk.

If the characters investigate the desk, they find a large tome lying closed upon it amid the art supplies, with a bookmark placed almost in the center. Opening the book anywhere other than the bookmark releases a trap: Roaches boil forth and form a **composite roach demon**.

Composite Demon (Roach): HD 2; **HP** 12; **AC** 4[15]; **Atk** smother (1d4); **Move** 9; **Save** 16; **AL** C; **CL/XP** 4/120; **Special**: resist bladed weapons (50% damage), smother (1d4 damage every round after successful hit, save avoids continuous damage; damage ends if demon is killed or attacks a different opponent). (see **Appendix B: New Monsters and Hazards**).

Opening the book to the bookmarked page reveals the following text (**Handout E**):

> *To open the room of the helm, the words are Yamatar, Vothontar, Uanibaster. Remember the interstice, for gaps are holy to the demon-princess.To resolve the ship into a dimension it occupies only partially, speak the words Phanoris, Temporis, Anchoris while in the room of the helm. Remember the interstice. The ship will not remain in place for more than an hour unless the words are spoken a second time.*

This information is required for the characters to enter the ship's control room and bring the ship into the proper phase with the Material Plane to escape. The words must be spoken in the magic circle in **Area 8**. If they are spoken anywhere other than in **Area 8**, it is clear that they have some magical effect, for nearby lights flicker and the person who speaks the words feels an odd, shifting sensation, but there is no other effect. Also, the "trap" in these words (the middle word is not actually supposed to be said aloud) is not a risk if the words are spoken outside of **Area 8**.

13. Cavern of the Petrified

Your initial impression of this chamber is that the floor is made of uneven masses of stone and that the area is filled with stalactites and stalagmites that join in the center to form irregularly shaped pillars. However, as the light plays onto the stone longer, you can see that the pillars and the lumps on the floor seem to be made of hundreds of thousands of smaller stones rather than being a normal limestone formation.

On further inspection, the component "rocks" are actually petrified roaches in the millions that create the rock formations. Even closer inspection reveals that the stone roaches are actually moving, but so slowly that the shifting of the formations happens only at a glacial pace.

The only way to explore the room is by breaking up into single file to get through the petrified-but-still-moving roaches. There is nothing dangerous in the chamber, and exploration quickly reveals the two additional interstice leading from the room. Unlike the others, these are formed of the stone roaches rather than by human skulls.

13A. Interstice from Area 9C

This cylinder is made of human skulls.

Refer to **Area 6A** for details on the interstices.
Walking through this interstice leads to **Area 9C**

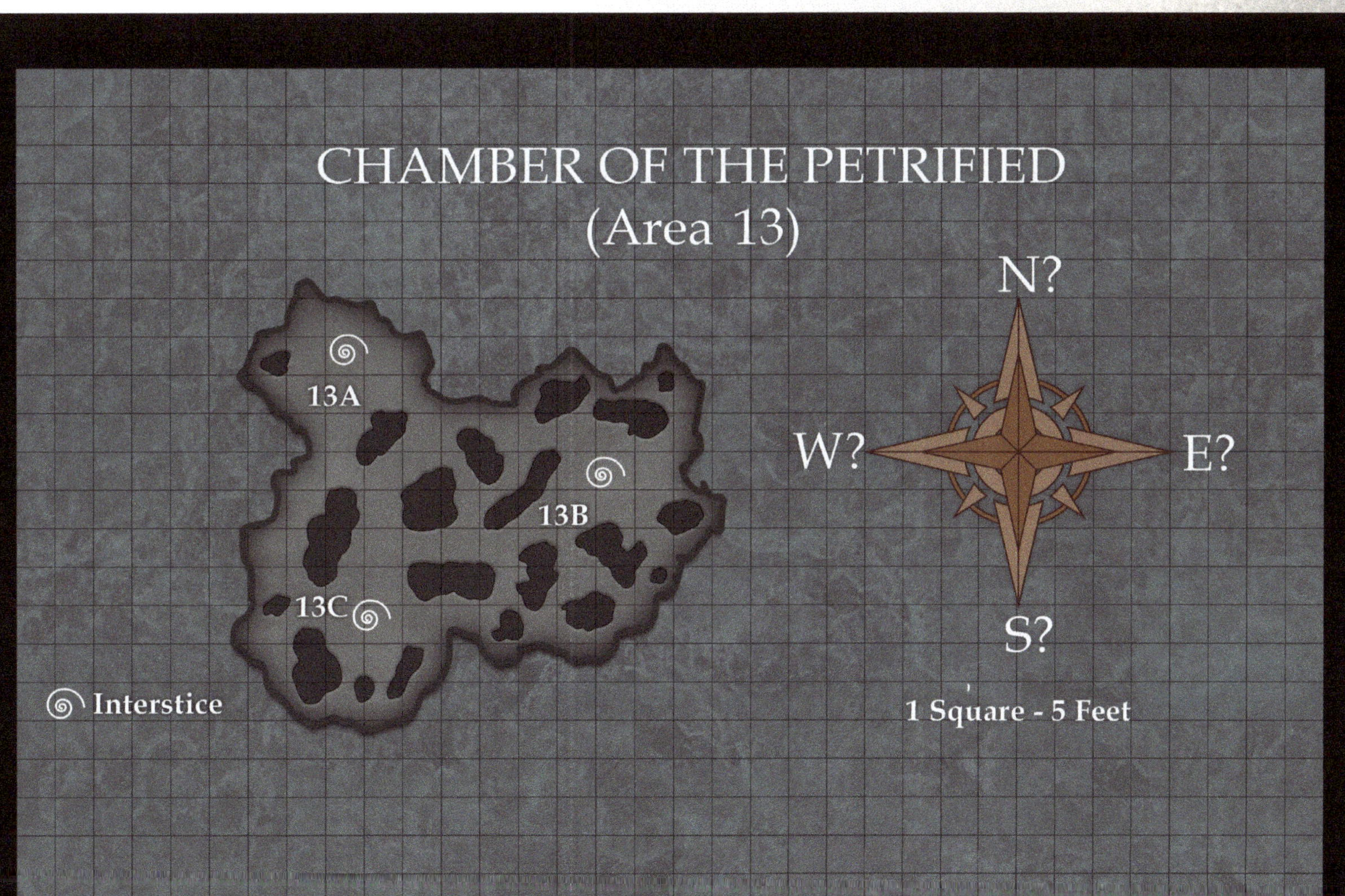

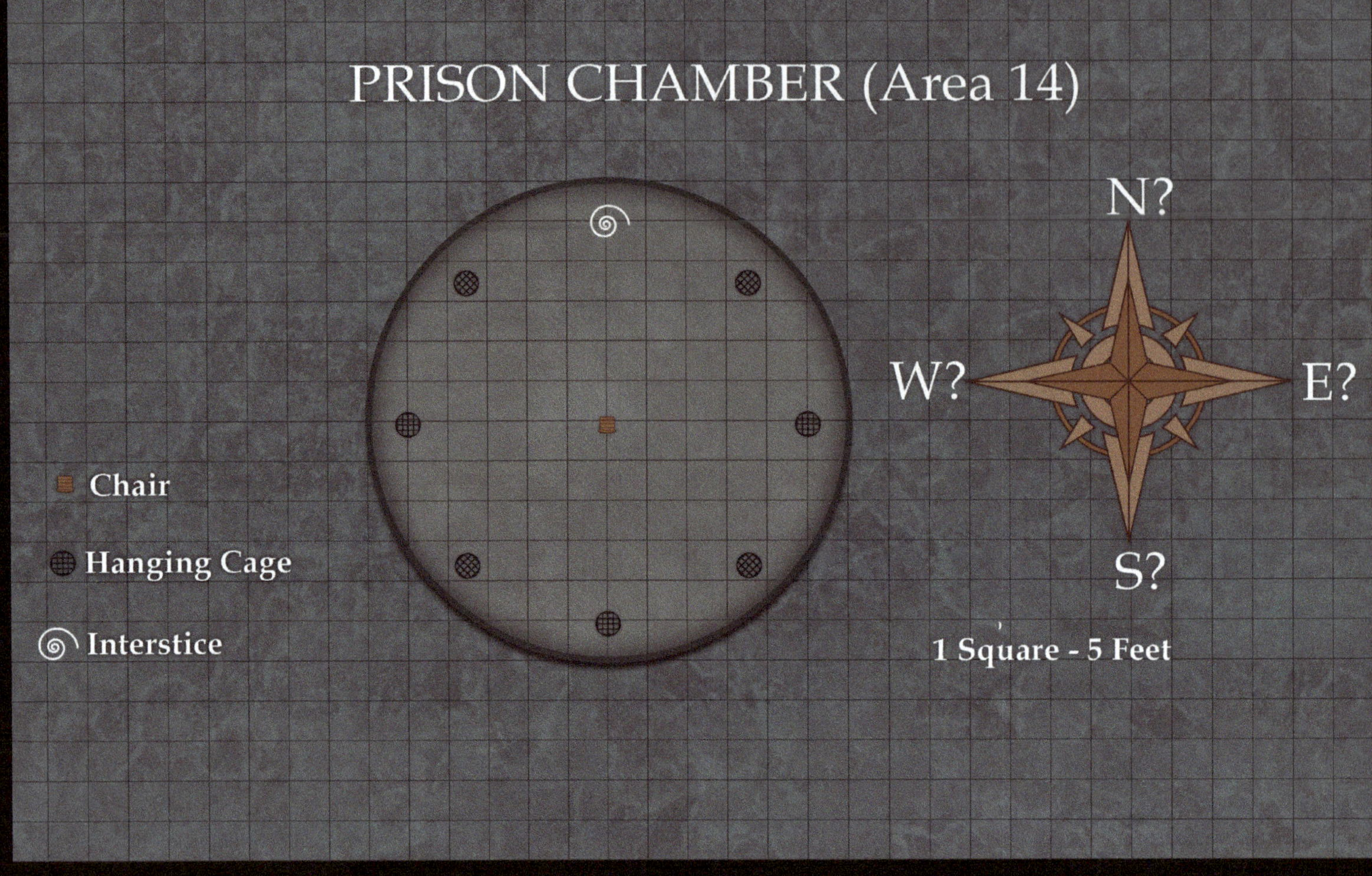

13B. Interstice to Area 10E (Counterclockwise)

This is a cylinder with a (counterclockwise) passage spiraling into it, like the others you have seen, but this one is not formed of human skulls. Rather, it is formed of the same material as the rest of the chamber: millions of slowly moving stone cockroaches.

Refer to **Area 6A** for details on the interstices.
Walking through this interstice leads to **Area 10E**.

13C. Interstice to Area 14 (Clockwise)

This is a cylinder with a (clockwise) passage spiraling into it, like the others you have seen, but this one is not formed of human skulls. Rather, it is formed of the same material as the rest of the chamber: millions of slowly moving stone cockroaches.

This interstice leads to **Area 14**.

14. Prison Chamber

This room has a large central chamber with a number of cages hanging from the ceiling. You don't have much of a chance to look at the details, though, because the room also contains a large man sitting on a wooden chair. He leaps to his feet when you emerge.

The Jailer: HD 3+1; **HP** 21; **AC** 5[14]; **Atk** club (1d4+1); **Move** 9; **Save** 14; **AL** C; **CL/XP** 3/60; **Special**: none.

The Prisoners

Either one or two prisoners are in the cages, depending on whether the characters already ran through *The Fiend of Turlin's Well*. If they did and the Fiend escaped, he is here in one of the cages. If not, then the only prisoner in the cages is Paravas Jaune.

Paravas Jaune:

Paravas Jaune is the son of a merchant in the city. His father pays well for his release (1,000 gp). He has overheard a fair amount of information about *The Shifting Fortune*, which makes him quite sure he is not being held for ransom but that a much more horrible fate awaits him.

Paravas is an intelligent, well-educated fellow familiar with the economy and political factions of Bard's Gate. Unfortunately, this sort of information was exactly what the crew of *The Shifting Fortune* needed, as no one on the vessel is even native to this plane of existence. Paravas was kidnapped in the city immediately after *The Shifting Fortune* first arrived and was interrogated by Torad Yarog and Lyuul the Roach for several days to give them information about the city and its environs. The two minions of the demon-princess spoke freely in front of him, which is how he knows they have no plans to release him.

Paravas Jaune, Normal Human Merchant: HP 2; **AC** 9[10]; **Atk** weapon (1d6); **Move** 12; **Save** 18; **AL** N; **CL/XP** B/10; **Special:** none. (*Monstrosities* 254)

The following is a list of information Paravas can disclose to the characters. He parses it out slowly until the characters agree to rescue him since it is the only bargaining chip he has.

- The ship is commanded by two people: Torad Yarog and Lyuul the Roach. Torad's face shifts to resemble different people at will, and his personality seems to change when he is frustrated. Lyuul wears a red robe and is a priest of some kind.
- Both of the two commanders seem to worship someone named "Teratashia." Paravas does not have the religious education to recognize the name; he just noticed that they use the word the same way people refer to their deities.
- At one point recently, Lyuul asked a series of questions about places in the city where a person might get arrested or lost, and Torad Yarog was not with him. During this visit, Lyuul said to the jailer, "He probably changed personalities into one that's not stable. If he's the fiend right now, we'll probably be able to track him by following the bodies."

The Fiend (Torad Yarog):

If the characters played through *The Fiend of Turlin's Well* and the Fiend escaped them, he is in this room, utterly insane. He returned to the ship after the adventure, and Lyuul placed him here until his personality shifts away from the Fiend and back into one of the more reliable personas.

Torad Yarog, the Fiend, Doppelganger (MU2): HD 4; **HP** 25; **AC** 5[14]; **Atk** claw (1d12); **Move** 9; **Save** 13 (5 vs. magic); **CL/XP** 6/400; **Special:** +5 save vs. magic, immune to sleep and charm, mimic shape, spells (2). (*Monstrosities* 129)

Spells: 1st—*charm person, magic missile*.

Note: Torad Yarog has multiple personalities, with one usually taking control at any given time. If he is present, his normal equipment has been taken from him.

15. THE CHAMBER OF THE HELM

You are standing on what appears to be a stone disk, 100 feet in diameter. In the center of the disk is an ornate helmet standing on a stone pedestal. Beyond the edges of the stone disk, you are looking out into clouds of oily purple-and-green mist that drifts slowly to reveal gaps. These gaps reveal a number of different landscapes. The most prominent of these is a view of the city, as seen from the prow of *The Shifting Fortune*. Others include a river with two giant stone pillars rising from the water, a castle on a hill under siege, and what appears to be an empty throne room of some kind.

This place is the locus of control for *The Shifting Fortune*, an interdimensional gap tied to the physical ship, its component interdimensional parts, and also to Teratashia's (currently unoccupied) throne room. The city is currently in view because it is where the physical ship is located, the two pillars are the Pillars of Draloon (where the ship is headed for its next voyage through the dimensions), the castle under siege is a random view, and the throne room is a view of the inside of Teratashia's palace in the underworld.

The helmet is the *Helm of The Shifting Fortune*, a magic item that is tied in its functioning to the ship and to the Demon-Princess Teratashia. The helm is what holds together all of the different dimensionally-separate parts of the ship, and it cannot be removed from this chamber.

USING THE HELM

To give commands to the ship, one of the characters must be wearing the helm, which responds to spoken commands.

Phanoris, Temporis, Anchoris: This command causes the ship to resolve itself fully into the Material Plane of Existence for the period of one hour (allowing the characters to gather up treasure and to escape without suffering the Zeno's paradox effect that keeps them here). Speaking the words a second time causes the ship to remain indefinitely; speaking them a third time causes the ship to move into partial resolution (its current state); and speaking them a fourth time causes the ship to move into the gaps between realities — more on this later.

Yamatar, Vothontar, Uanibaster: This command (normally used to enter the helm chamber) does not affect anyone wearing the helm, as the helm is an integral part of the chamber. The command will, however, banish anyone *else* in the chamber back to **Area 8**. If the words are spoken when no one is in the chamber (other than the person wearing the helm), it summons anyone in the magic circle in **Area 8** into the chamber.

Bedoriomedes. Omniphonologon. Anjoole: Speaking these words while wearing the helm unlocks the door in **Area 12**.

The ship can move into dimensional gaps only when it is located at a gateway, so if the characters speak the words four times, there will not be any effect unless they piloted the ship to the Pillars of Draloon. If they do so and then speak the words four times, they embark upon a major adventure that is most likely far above their level of experience. From that point on, if they are that set on taking the risk, it is left to you to manage what happens to them in their new role as dimensional explorers in possession of a demonic artifact, pursued by the minions of a vengeful demon-princess.

It is more likely that they are focused entirely on escaping the ship, in which case their best course of action is to speak the words once or twice (anchoring the ship), stack whatever treasure they have into a boat, and escape.

CONCLUDING THE ADVENTURE

One definite loose end remains, which is the group of crewmembers who are on shore looking for the Fiend. Four of these cultists are roaming around the city. If the characters settle into *The Shifting Fortune* with the intention of adventuring through the dimensions, the four cultists arrive back at the ship after the characters have been there for roughly five days. It is definitely possible that the characters could deceive the cultists into believing that they are continuing Teratashia's will — after all, takeovers and changes of command aren't uncommon in the hierarchy of demonic cultists. The cultists are ultimately not terribly important, so use them as a tool to move your game forward, not as an anticlimactic loose end to tie up.

IT IS SAID that the Demon-Princess Teratashia's dark palace in the depths of the Abyss is a nexus of countless gaps between dimensions, a warren of tunnels worming their way deep into a multitude of other realities. From the center of this web of connections, Teratashia sends her minions creeping and slithering through the planes of existence to do her bidding. Her motives and methods are inscrutable, for the demon-princess seldom involves herself in the quarrels of the other great demons. She is far more interested in controlling the nooks and crannies between dimensions than with her political status in the Abyss. She is inclined to leave the other demon princes alone to the same degree that they also extend that courtesy to her.

From the imagery of her statues and temples, Teratashia resembles a huge, female-headed cockroach with a feral visage, wearing a necklace of human skulls.

The author takes note that very little is truly known about this demon-princess.

For Teratashia is the Princess Between, the watcher where there is nothing, the traveler in emptiness, the crawler of wormholes, the finder of lost places, Demon-Princess of the Unseen.

She rules the spaces where naught exists, the pathways through nothing, and finds the ways between.

She watches, listens, finds, takes, feeds, with feral face and chitin wings, for she is the Roach Queen.

<u>ORDERS</u>
SHIP TO TAKE PASSAGE THROUGH THE PILLARS OF
DRALOON AND THENCE INTO THE GAP OF GESTRIA.
UPON THE DEATH OF THE OARSMEN IN THE GAP,
THENCE TO THE UNDERWORLD OF MAUG, TO
DELIVER ONE SACRED EGG AND TAKE ON A
CARGO OF PORTABLE HOLES

BEDORIOMEDES.OMNIPHONOLOGON.ANJOOLE

—To open the room of the <u>HELM</u> the words are:
Yamatar, Vothontar, Uanibaster
Remember the interstice, for gaps are holy
to the demon-princess

— To resolve the ship into a dimension it
occupies only partially, speak the words

Phanoris, Temporis, Anchoris while in
the room of the HELM. Remember the
interstice. The ship will not remain
in place for more than an hour unless
the words are spoken a second time.

Appendix B: New Monsters and Hazards

Composite Demon (Roach)

Composite demons are one of the signature minions of the Demon-Princess Teratashia. These swarms of verminous creatures are possessed by one of her lesser demons. The demons are almost immaterial when they are not in possession of a swarm, although they do have a smoke-like appearance in Teratashia's underworlds and the gaps between planes where she exerts her presence.

Hit Dice: 2
Armor Class: 4[15]
Attacks: Smother (1d4)
Saving Throw: 16
Special: Smother, half damage from bladed weapons
Move: 9 (as swarm)
Alignment: Chaos
Number Encountered: Varies
Challenge Level/XP: 4/120

The demon forms its possessed swarm of roaches into a vaguely humanoid form, which lashes out with its arms and seeks to grab victims in a suffocating hug of cockroaches. When the demon hits, it begins to smother the victim, inflicting 1d4 points of damage per round unless the victim makes a saving throw. The attack continues without the need to make a to-hit roll until the demon is killed or breaks off to attack a different opponent.

Due to their composite form, these demons take only half damage from bladed weapons.

Composite Demon (Roach): HD 2; AC 4[15]; Atk smother (1d4); **Move** 9; **Save** 16; **AL** C; **CL/XP** 4/120; **Special**: resist bladed weapons (50% damage), smother (1d4 damage every round after successful hit, save avoids continuous damage; damage ends if demon is killed or attacks a different opponent).

Cultist of Teratashia

Hit Dice: 2
Armor Class: 5[14]
Attacks: Mace (1d4+1)
Saving Throw: 15
Special: None
Move: 9
Alignment: Chaos
Number Encountered: Varies
Challenge Level/XP: 2/30

Cultists of Teratashia are all vaguely human-seeming in appearance, but they are recruited in a number of different ports throughout the dimensions and planes of existence, so they never look entirely normal wherever they appear in the service of their mistress.

Cultist of Teratashia: HD 2; AC 5[14]; Atk mace (1d4+1); **Move** 9; **Save** 15; **AL** C; **CL/XP** 2/30; **Special**: none.

Non-Matter

Non-matter is a black, tarry substance that bubbles slowly.

Anything touching it evaporates into nothingness, as if it made contact with the strongest of acid. No material substance is immune to the effect, including gases. An incorporeal being is not annihilated by contact, but faces a different problem — since the black tar holds together the ship's component structure in a sea of nothingness, an incorporeal being touching the non-matter is pulled outward into the void of interplanar space and lost forever. So, it isn't much better, really.

A character who touches the tar takes 1d6 points of damage, or half damage if the character makes a saving throw. A second exposure causes 2d6 points of damage, while a third causes 3d6 points of damage, and so on. The stuff is lethal, and since it cannot be contained in any material barrier (it oozes out slowly), it cannot be put to use as a weapon.

Appendix C: Demons, Divinities, and Artifacts

Charon of Far Kathan

Charon of Far Kathan is a quasi-deity of a distant dimension related to the ordinary Charon with which the characters may be familiar. This deity's cult centers around the concept of breaking off filled crypts from their home dimension for the journey into the underworld.

Teratashia

Background Information for the Referee)Teratashia resembles a huge, female-headed cockroach with a feral visage who wears a necklace of human skulls. She is the Demon-Princess of Dimensions and Gaps, and as such is one of the major powers in the Between.

Her dark palace is located in the depths of the Abyss — a nexus of countless gaps between dimensions, of tunnels worming their way deep into a multitude of other realities. From the center of this web of connections, Teratashia sends her minions creeping and slithering through the planes of existence to do her bidding. Her motives and methods are inscrutable, for the demon-princess seldom involves herself in the quarrels of the other great demons. She is far more interested in controlling the nooks and crannies between dimensions than with her political status in the Abyss. She is inclined to leave the other demon princes alone to the same degree that they also extend that courtesy to her.

The Shifting Fortune (Artifact)

The Shifting Fortune is an extremely powerful artifact, and unless you want to take the campaign into a planar-adventuring context, it is the sort of thing that is too dangerous to hold onto. Many powerful creatures would love to get their hands on something like this, and the Demon-Princess Teratashia is certain to want it back. The ship's "navigation" is currently done by Teratashia's direct intervention (hence the code words being recorded in writing by the captain), and the characters would need some way of telling the ship where to go if you decide to take the campaign in that direction. The most likely candidate for this would be an NPC with experience having to do with the planes of existence … if the characters can trust someone with that sort of knowledge.

FROG GOD
GAMES
ADVENTURES
WORTH WINNING